The Bickerstaff-Partridge Papers

The Bickerstaff-Partridge Papers

Jonathan Swift

MINT EDITIONS

The Bickerstaff-Partridge Papers was first published in 1708.

This edition published by Mint Editions 2020.

ISBN 9781513270302 | E-ISBN 9781513275307

Published by Mint Editions®

 MINT
EDITIONS

minteditionbooks.com

Publishing Director: Jennifer Newens
Design & Production: Rachel Lopez Metzger
Project Manager: Micaela Clark
Typesetting: Westchester Publishing Services

Predictions For The Year 1708

Wherein the month, and day of the month are set down, the persons named, and the great actions and events of next year particularly related, as will come to pass.

Written to prevent the people of England from being farther imposed on by vulgar almanack-makers.

By Isaac Bickerstaff, Esq.

I have long consider'd the gross abuse of astrology in this kingdom, and upon debating the matter with myself, I could not possibly lay the fault upon the art, but upon those gross impostors, who set up to be the artists. I know several learned men have contended that the whole is a cheat; that it is absurd and ridiculous to imagine, the stars can have any influence at all upon human actions, thoughts, or inclinations: And whoever has not bent his studies that way, may be excused for thinking so, when he sees in how wretched a manner that noble art is treated by a few mean illiterate traders between us and the stars; who import a yearly stock of nonsense, lyes, folly, and impertinence, which they offer to the world as genuine from the planets, tho' they descend from no greater a height than their own brains.

I intend in a short time to publish a large and rational defence of this art, and therefore shall say no more in its justification at present, than that it hath been in all ages defended by many learned men, and among the rest by Socrates himself, whom I look upon as undoubtedly the wisest of uninspir'd mortals: To which if we add, that those who have condemned this art, though otherwise learned, having been such as either did not apply their studies this way, or at least did not succeed in their applications; their testimony will not be of much weight to its disadvantage, since they are liable to the common objection of condemning what they did not understand.

Nor am I at all offended, or think it an injury to the art, when I see the common dealers in it, the students in astrology, the philomaths, and the rest of that tribe, treated by wise men with the utmost scorn and contempt; but rather wonder, when I observe gentlemen in the country, rich enough to serve the nation in parliament, poring in Partridge's almanack, to find out the events of the year at home and abroad; not daring to propose a hunting-match, till Gadbury or he have fixed the weather.

I will allow either of the two I have mentioned, or any other of the fraternity, to be not only astrologers, but conjurers too, if I do not produce a hundred instances in all their almanacks, to convince any reasonable man, that they do not so much as understand common grammar and syntax; that they are not able to spell any word out of the usual road, nor even in their prefaces write common sense or intelligible English. Then for their observations and predictions, they are such as will equally suit any age or country in the world. "This month a certain great person will be threatened with death or sickness." This the news-papers will tell them; for there we find at the end of the year, that no month passes without the death of some person of note; and it would be hard if it should be otherwise, when there are at least two thousand persons of not in this kingdom, many of them old, and the almanack-maker has the liberty of chusing the sickliest season of the year where he may fix his prediction. Again, "This month an eminent clergyman will be preferr'd;" of which there may be some hundreds half of them with one foot in the grave. Then "such a planet in such a house shews great machinations, plots and conspiracies, that may in time be brought to light:" After which, if we hear of any discovery, the astrologer gets the honour; if not, his prediction still stands good. And at last, "God preserve King William from all his open and secret enemies, Amen." When if the King should happen to have died, the astrologer plainly foretold it; otherwise it passes but for the pious ejaculation of a loyal subject: Though it unluckily happen'd in some of their almanacks, that poor King William was pray'd for many months after he was dead, because it fell out that he died about the beginning of the year.

To mention no more of their impertinent predictions: What have we to do with their advertisements about pills and drink for the venereal disease? Or their mutual quarrels in verse and prose of Whig and Tory, wherewith the stars have little to do?

Having long observed and lamented these, and a hundred other abuses of this art, too tedious to repeat, I resolved to proceed in a new way, which I doubt not will be to the general satisfaction of the kingdom: I can this year produce but a specimen of what I design for the future; having employ'd most part of my time in adjusting and correcting the calculations I made some years past, because I would offer nothing to the world of which I am not as fully satisfied, as that I am now alive.

For these two last years I have not failed in above one or two particulars, and those of no very great moment. I exactly foretold the miscarriage at Toulon, with all its particulars; and the loss of Admiral Shovel, tho' I was mistaken as to the day, placing that accident about thirty-six hours sooner than it happen'd; but upon reviewing my schemes, I quickly found the cause of that error. I likewise foretold the Battle of Almanza to the very day and hour, with the loss on both sides, and the consequences thereof. All which I shewed to some friends many months before they happened, that is, I gave them papers sealed up, to open at such a time, after which they were at liberty to read them; and there they found my predictions true in every article, except one or two, very minute.

As for the few following predictions I now offer the world, I forbore to publish them till I had perused the several almanacks for the year we are now enter'd on. I find them in all the usual strain, and I beg the reader will compare their manner with mine: And here I make bold to tell the world, that I lay the whole credit of my art upon the truth of these predictions; and I will be content, that Partridge, and the rest of his clan, may hoot me for a cheat and impostor, if I fail in any singular particular of moment. I believe, any man who reads this paper, will look upon me to be at least a person of as much honesty and understanding, as a common maker of almanacks. I do not lurk in the dark; I am not wholly unknown in the world; I have set my name at length, to be a mark of infamy to mankind, if they shall find I deceive them.

In one thing I must desire to be forgiven, that I talk more sparingly of home-affairs: As it will be imprudence to discover secrets of state, so it would be dangerous to my person; but in smaller matters, and that are not of publick consequence, I shall be very free; and the truth of my conjectures will as much appear from those as the other. As for the most signal events abroad in France, Flanders, Italy and Spain, I shall make no scruple to predict them in plain terms: Some of them are of importance, and I hope I shall seldom mistake the day they will happen; therefore, I think good to inform the reader, that I all along make use of the Old Style observed in England, which I desire he will compare with that of the news-papers, at the time they relate the actions I mention.

I must add one word more: I know it hath been the opinion of several of the learned, who think well enough of the true art of astrology, That the stars do only incline, and not force the actions or wills of men: And therefore, however I may proceed by right rules, yet I cannot in prudence so confidently assure the events will follow exactly as I predict them.

I hope I have maturely considered this objection, which in some cases is of no little weight. For example: A man may, by the influence of an over-ruling planet, be disposed or inclined to lust, rage, or avarice, and yet by the force of reason overcome that bad influence; and this was the case of Socrates: But as the great events of the world usually depend upon numbers of men, it cannot be expected they should all unite to cross their inclinations, from pursuing a general design, wherein they unanimously agree. Besides the influence of the stars reaches to many actions and events which are not any way in the power of reason; as sickness, death, and what we commonly call accidents, with many more, needless to repeat.

But now it is time to proceed to my predictions, which I have begun to calculate from the time that the Sun enters into Aries. And this I take to be properly the beginning of the natural year. I pursue them to the time that he enters Libra, or somewhat more, which is the busy period of the year. The remainder I have not yet adjusted, upon account of several impediments needless here to mention: Besides, I must remind the reader again, that this is but a specimen of what I design in succeeding years to treat more at large, if I may have liberty and encouragement.

My first prediction is but a trifle, yet I will mention it, to show how ignorant those sottish pretenders to astrology are in their own concerns: It relates to Partridge the almanack-maker; I have consulted the stars of his nativity by my own rules, and find he will infallibly die upon the 29th of March next, about eleven at night, of a raging fever; therefore I advise him to consider of it, and settle his affairs in time.

The month of April will be observable for the death of many great persons. On the 4th will die the Cardinal de Noailles, Archbishop of Paris: On the 11th the young Prince of Asturias, son to the Duke of Anjou: On the 14th a great peer of this realm will die at his country-house: On the 19th an old layman of great fame for learning: and on the 23rd an eminent goldsmith in Lombard-Street. I could mention others, both at home and abroad, if I did not consider it is of very little use or instruction to the reader, or to the world.

As to publick affairs: On the 7th of this month there will be an insurrection in Dauphine, occasion'd by the oppressions of the people, which will not be quieted in some months.

On the 15th will be a violent storm on the south-east coast of France, which will destroy many of their ships, and some in the very harbour.

The 19th will be famous for the revolt of a whole province or kingdom, excepting one city, by which the affairs of a certain prince in the alliance will take a better face.

May, against common conjectures, will be no very busy month in Europe, but very signal for the death of the Dauphin, which will happen on the 7th, after a short fit of sickness, and grievous torments with the strangury. He dies less lamented by the court than the kingdom.

On the 9th a Mareschal of France will break his leg by a fall from his horse. I have not been able to discover whether he will then die or not.

On the 11th will begin a most important siege, which the eyes of all Europe will be upon: I cannot be more particular: for in relating affairs that so nearly concern the Confederates, and consequently this Kingdom, I am forced to confine myself, for several reasons very obvious to the reader.

On the 15th news will arrive of a very surprizing event, than which nothing could be more unexpected.

On the 19th three noble ladies of this Kingdom will, against all expectation, prove with child, to the great joy of their husbands.

On the 23rd a famous buffoon of the play-house will die a ridiculous death, suitable to his vocation.

June. This month will be distinguish'd at home, by the utter dispersing of those ridiculous deluded enthusiasts, commonly call'd the Prophets; occasion'd chiefly by seeing the time come that many of their prophecies should be fulfill'd, and then finding themselves deceiv'd by contrary events. It is indeed to be admir'd how any deceiver can be so weak, to foretel things near at hand, when a very few months must of necessity discover the impostor to all the world; in this point less prudent than common almanack-makers, who are so wise to wonder in generals, and talk dubiously, and leave to the reader the business of interpreting.

On the 1st of this month a French general will be killed by a random shot of a cannon-ball.

On the 6th a fire will break out in the suburbs of Paris, which will destroy above a thousand houses; and seems to be the foreboding of what will happen, to the surprize of all Europe, about the end of the following month.

On the 10th a great battle will be fought, which will begin at four of the clock in the afternoon; and last till nine at night with great obstinacy, but no very decisive event. I shall not name the place, for the reasons aforesaid; but the commanders on each left wing will be killed.—I see bonfires, and hear the noise of guns for a victory.

On the 14th there will be a false report of the French king's death.

On the 20th Cardinal Portocarero will die of a dysentery, with great suspicion of poison; but the report of his intention to revolt to King Charles, will prove false.

July. The 6th of this month a certain general will, by a glorious action, recover the reputation he lost by former misfortunes.

On the 12th a great commander will die a prisoner in the hands of his enemies.

On the 14th a shameful discovery will be made of a French Jesuit, giving poison to a great foreign general; and when he is put to the torture, will make wonderful discoveries.

In short this will prove a month of great action, if I might have liberty to relate the particulars.

At home, the death of an old famous senator will happen on the 15th at his country-house, worn with age and diseases.

But that which will make this month memorable to all posterity, is the death of the French King, Lewis the fourteenth, after a week's sickness at Marli, which will happen on the 29th, about six o'clock in the evening. It seems to be an effect of the gout in his stomach, followed by a flux. And in three days after Monsieur Chamillard will follow his master, dying suddenly of an appoplexy.

In this month likewise an ambassador will die in London; but I cannot assign the day.

August. The affairs of France will seem to suffer no change for a while under the Duke of Burgundy's administration; but the genius that animated the whole machine being gone, will be the cause of mighty turns and revolutions in the following year. The new King makes yet little change either in the army or the ministry; but the libels against his grandfather, that fly about his very court, give him uneasiness.

I see an express in mighty haste, with joy and wonder in his looks, arriving by break of day on the 26th of this month, having travell'd in three days a prodigious journey by land and sea. In the evening I hear bells and guns, and see the blazing of a thousand bonfires.

A young admiral of noble birth, does likewise this month gain immortal honour by a great achievement.

The affairs of Poland are this month entirely settled: Augustus resigns his pretensions which he had again taken up for some time:

Stanislaus is peaceably possess'd of the throne; and the King of Sweden declares for the Emperor.

I cannot omit one particular accident here at home; that near the end of this month much mischief will be done at Bartholomew Fair, by the fall of a booth.

September. This month begins with a very surprizing fit of frosty weather, which will last near twelve days.

The Pope having long languish'd last month, the swellings in his legs breaking, and the flesh mortifying, will die on the 11th instant; and in three weeks time, after a mighty contest, be succeeded by a cardinal of the imperial faction, but native of Tuscany, who is now about sixty-one years old.

The French army acts now wholly on the defensive, strongly fortify'd in their trenches; and the young French King sends overtures for a treaty of peace by the Duke of Mantua; which, because it is a matter of state that concerns us here at home, I shall speak no farther of it.

I shall add but one prediction more, and that in mystical terms, which shall be included in a verse out of Virgil,

Alter erit jam Tethys, & altera quae vehat Argo. Delectos heroas.

Upon the 25th day of this month, the fulfilling of this prediction will be manifest to every body.

This is the farthest I have proceeded in my calculations for the present year. I do not pretend, that these are all the great events which will happen in this period, but that those I have set down will infallibly come to pass. It will perhaps still be objected, why I have not spoke more particularly of affairs at home, or of the success of our armies abroad, which I might, and could very largely have done; but those in power have wisely discouraged men from meddling in publick concerns, and I was resolv'd by no means to give the least offence. This I will venture to say, That it will be a glorious campaign for the allies, wherein the English forces, both by sea and land, will have their full share of honour: That her Majesty Queen Anne will continue in health and prosperity: And that no ill accident will arrive to any of the chief ministry.

As to the particular events I have mention'd, the readers may judge by the fulfilling of 'em, whether I am on the level with common astrologers; who, with an old paultry cant, and a few pothook for planets, to amuse the vulgar, have, in my opinion, too long been suffer'd to abuse the world: But an honest physician ought not to be despis'd, because there are such things as mountebanks. I hope I have some share of reputation, which

I would not willingly forfeit for a frolick or humour: And I believe no gentleman, who reads this paper, will look upon it to be of the same cast or mould with the common scribblers that are every day hawk'd about. My fortune has placed me above the little regard of scribbling for a few pence, which I neither value or want: Therefore let no wise men too hastily condemn this essay, intended for a good design, to cultivate and improve an ancient art, long in disgrace, by having fallen into mean and unskilful hands. A little time will determine whether I have deceived others or myself: and I think it is no very unreasonable request, that men would please to suspend their judgments till then. I was once of the opinion with those who despise all predictions from the stars, till the year 1686, a man of quality shew'd me, written in his album, That the most learned astronomer, Captain H. assured him, he would never believe any thing of the stars' influence, if there were not a great revolution in England in the year 1688. Since that time I began to have other thoughts, and after eighteen years diligent study and application, I think I have no reason to repent of my pains. I shall detain the reader no longer, than to let him know, that the account I design to give of next year's events, shall take in the principal affairs that happen in Europe; and if I be denied the liberty of offering it to my own country, I shall appeal to the learned world, by publishing it in Latin, and giving order to have it printed in Holland.

*   *   *   *   *

The Accomplishment of the First of Mr. Bickerstaff's Predictions;

being an account of the death of Mr. Partridge, the almanack-maker, upon the 29th instant.

In a letter to a person of honour Written in the year 1708

> My Lord,
>   In obedience to your Lordship's commands, as well as to satisfy my own curiosity, I have for some days past enquired constantly after Partridge the almanack-maker, of whom it was foretold in Mr. Bickerstaff's predictions, publish'd about a month ago, that he should die on the 29th instant about eleven at night of a raging fever. I had some sort of knowledge of him when I was employ'd in the Revenue, because he used every year to present me with his almanack, as he did other gentlemen, upon the score of some little

gratuity we gave him. I saw him accidentally once or twice about ten days before he died, and observed he began very much to droop and languish, tho' I hear his friends did not seem to apprehend him in any danger. About two or three days ago he grew ill, and was confin'd first to his chamber, and in a few hours after to his bed, where Dr. Case and Mrs. Kirleus were sent for to visit, and to prescribe to him. Upon this intelligence I sent thrice every day one servant or other to enquire after his health; and yesterday, about four in the afternoon, word was brought me that he was past hopes: Upon which, I prevailed with myself to go and see him, partly out of commiseration, and I confess, partly out of curiosity. He knew me very well, seem'd surpriz'd at my condescension, and made me compliments upon it as well as he could, in the condition he was. The people about him said, he had been for some time delirious; but when I saw him, he had his understanding as well as ever I knew, and spake strong and hearty, without any seeming uneasiness or constraint. After I told him how sorry I was to see him in those melancholy circumstances, and said some other civilities, suitable to the occasion, I desired him to tell me freely and ingeniously, whether the predictions Mr. Bickerstaff had publish'd relating to his death, had not too much affected and worked on his imagination. He confess'd he had often had it in his head, but never with much apprehension, till about a fortnight before; since which time it had the perpetual possession of his mind and thoughts, and he did verily believe was the true natural cause of his present distemper: For, said he, I am thoroughly persuaded, and I think I have very good reasons, that Mr. Bickerstaff spoke altogether by guess, and knew no more what will happen this year than I did myself. I told him his discourse surprized me; and I would be glad he were in a state of health to be able to tell me what reason he had to be convinc'd of Mr. Bickerstaff's ignorance. He reply'd, I am a poor ignorant fellow, bred to a mean trade, yet I have sense enough to know that all pretences of foretelling by astrology are deceits, for this manifest reason, because the wise and the learned, who can only know whether there be any truth in this science, do all unanimously agree to laugh at and despise it; and none but the poor ignorant vulgar give it any credit, and that only upon the word of such silly wretches as I and my fellows, who can hardly write or read. I then asked him why he had not calculated his own nativity, to see whether it agreed with Bickerstaff's prediction? at which he shook his head, and said, Oh! sir, this is no time for jesting, but for repenting those fooleries, as I do now from the very bottom of my heart. By what I can gather from you, said I, the observations and predictions you printed, with your almanacks, were mere impositions on the people. He reply'd, if it were otherwise I should have the less to answer for. We have a common form for all those things, as to foretelling the weather, we never meddle with that, but leave it to the printer, who takes it out of any old almanack, as he thinks fit; the rest was my own invention, to make my almanack sell, having a wife to maintain, and no other way to get my bread; for mending old shoes is a poor livelihood; and, (added he, sighing) I wish I may not have done more mischief by my physick than my astrology; tho' I had some good receipts from my grandmother, and my own compositions were such as I thought could at least do no hurt.

I had some other discourse with him, which now I cannot call to mind; and I fear I have already tired your Lordship. I shall only add one circumstance, That on his death-bed he declared himself a Nonconformist, and had a fanatick preacher to be his spiritual guide. After half an hour's conversation I took my leave, being half stifled by the closeness of the room. I imagine he could not hold out long, and therefore withdrew to a little coffee-house hard by, leaving a servant at the house with orders to come immediately, and tell me, as near as he could, the minute when Partridge should expire, which was not above two hours after; when, looking upon my watch, I found it to be above five minutes after seven; by which it is clear that Mr. Bickerstaff was mistaken almost four hours in his calculation. In the other circumstances he was exact enough. But whether he has not been the cause of this poor man's death, as well as the predictor, may be very reasonably disputed. However, it must be confess'd the matter is odd enough, whether we should endeavour to account for it by chance, or the effect of imagination: For my own part, tho' I believe no man has less faith in these matters, yet I shall wait with some impatience, and not without some expectation, the fulfilling of Mr. Bickerstaff's second prediction, that the Cardinal de Noailles is to die upon the fourth of April, and if that should be verified as exactly as this of poor Partridge, I must own I should be wholly surprized, and at a loss, and should infallibly expect the accomplishment of all the rest.

* * * * *

An Elegy on the supposed Death of Partridge, the Almanack-Maker.

> *Well, 'tis as Bickerstaff has guess'd,*
> *Tho' we all took it for a jest;*
> *Partridge is dead, nay more, he dy'd*
> *E're he could prove the good 'Squire ly'd.*
> *Strange, an Astrologer shou'd die,*
> *Without one Wonder in the Sky!*
> *Not one of all his Crony Stars*
> *To pay their Duty at his Herse?*
> *No Meteor, no Eclipse appear'd?*
> *No Comet with a flaming Beard?*
> *The Sun has rose, and gone to Bed,*
> *Just as if partridge were not dead:*
> *Nor hid himself behind the Moon,*
> *To make a dreadful Night at Noon.*
> *He at fit Periods walks through Aries,*
> *Howe'er our earthly Motion varies;*
> *And twice a Year he'll cut th' Equator,*
> *As if there had been no such Matter.*
>
> *Some Wits have wonder'd what Analogy*
> *There is 'twixt Cobbling* and Astrology:*
> *How Partridge made his Optics rise,*
> *From a Shoe-Sole, to reach the Skies.*

---

* Partridge was a Cobler.

A List of Coblers Temples Ties,
To keep the Hair out of their Eyes;
From whence 'tis plain the Diadem
That Princes wear, derives from them.
And therefore Crowns are now-a-days
Adorn'd with Golden Stars and Rays,
Which plainly shews the near Alliance
'Twixt cobling and the Planets Science.

Besides, that slow-pac'd Sign Bootes,
As 'tis miscall'd, we know not who 'tis?
But Partridge ended all Disputes,
He knew his Trade, and call'd it *Boots.

The Horned Moon, which heretofore
Upon their Shoes the Romans wore,
Whose Wideness kept their Toes from Corns,
And whence we claim our Shooing-Horns;
Shows how the Art of Cobling bears
A near Resemblance to the Spheres.

A Scrap of Parchment hung by Geometry
(A great Refinement in Barometry)
Can, like the Stars, foretel the Weather;
And what is Parchment else but Leather?
Which an Astrologer might use,
Either for Almanacks or Shoes.

Thus Partridge, by his Wit and Parts,
At once did practise both these Arts;
And as the boading Owl (or rather
The Bat, because her Wings are Leather)
Steals from her private Cell by Night,
And flies about the Candle-Light;
So learned Partridge could as well
Creep in the Dark from Leathern Cell,
And, in his Fancy, fly as fair,
To peep upon a twinkling Star.

---

* See his Almanack

JONATHAN SWIFT

Besides, he could confound the Spheres,
And set the Planets by the Ears;
To shew his Skill, he Mars could join
To Venus in Aspect Mali'n;
Then call in Mercury for Aid,
And cure the Wounds that Venus made.

Great Scholars have in Lucian read,
When Philip, King of Greece was dead,
His Soul and Spirit did divide,
And each Part took a diff'rent Side;
One rose a Star, the other fell
Beneath, and mended Shoes in Hell.

Thus Partridge still shines in each Art,
The Cobling and Star-gazing Part,
And is install'd as good a Star
As any of the Caesars are.

Triumphant Star! some Pity shew
On Coblers militant below,
Whom roguish Boys in stormy Nights
Torment, by pissing out their Lights;
Or thro' a Chink convey their Smoke;
Inclos'd Artificers to choke.

Thou, high exalted in thy Sphere,
May'st follow still thy Calling there.
To thee the Bull will lend his hide,
By Phoebus newly tann'd and dry'd.
For thee they Argo's Hulk will tax,
And scrape her pitchy Sides for Wax.
Then Ariadne kindly lends
Her braided Hair to make thee Ends.
The Point of Sagittarius' Dart
Turns to an awl, by heav'nly Art;
And Vulcan, wheedled by his Wife,
Will forge for thee a Paring-Knife.
For want of Room, by Virgo's Side,

She'll strain a Point, and sit astride*,
To take thee kindly in between,
And then the Signs will be Thirteen.

*   *   *   *   *

An Epitaph on Partridge.

Here, five Foot deep, lies on his Back,
A Cobler, Starmonger, and Quack;
Who to the Stars in pure Good-will,
Does to his best look upward still.
Weep all you Customers that use
His Pills, his Almanacks, or Shoes;
And you that did your Fortunes seek,
Step to his Grave but once a Week:
This Earth which bears his Body's Print,
You'll find has so much Vertue in't,
That I durst pawn my Ears 'twill tell
Whate'er concerns you full as well,
In Physick, Stolen Goods, or Love,
As he himself could, when above.

*   *   *   *   *

Partridge's reply

'Squire Bickerstaff detected; or, the astrological impostor convicted;

by John Partridge, student in physick and astrology.

It is hard, my dear countrymen of these united nations, it is very hard that a Briton born, a Protestant astrologer, a man of revolution principles, an assertor of the liberty and property of the people, should cry out, in vain, for justice against a Frenchman, a Papist, an illiterate pretender to science; that would blast my reputation, most inhumanly bury me alive, and defraud my native country of those services, that, in my double capacity, I daily offer to the publick.

What great provocations I have receiv'd, let the impartial reader judge, and how unwillingly, even in my own defence, I now enter the

---

* Tibi brachia contrahet ingens Scorpius, etc.

lists against falsehood, ignorance and envy: But I am exasperated, at length, to drag out this cacus from the den of obscurity where he lurks, detect him by the light of those stars he has so impudently traduced, and shew there's not a monster in the skies so pernicious and malevolent to mankind, as an ignorant pretender to physick and astrology. I shall not directly fall on the many gross errors, nor expose the notorious absurdities of this prostituted libeller, till I have let the learned world fairly into the controversy depending, and then leave the unprejudiced to judge of the merits and justice of the cause.

It was towards the conclusion of the year 1707, when an impudent pamphlet crept into the world, intituled, 'Predictions, etc.' by Isaac Bickerstaff, Esq;—Amongst the many arrogant assertions laid down by that lying spirit of divination, he was pleas'd to pitch on the Cardinal de Noailles and myself, among many other eminent and illustrious persons, that were to die within the compass of the ensuing year; and peremptorily fixes the month, day, and hour of our deaths: This, I think, is sporting with great men, and publick spirits, to the scandal of religion, and reproach of power; and if sovereign princes and astrologers must make diversion for the vulgar— why then farewel, say I, to all governments, ecclesiastical and civil. But, I thank my better stars, I am alive to confront this false and audacious predictor, and to make him rue the hour he ever affronted a man of science and resentment. The Cardinal may take what measures he pleases with him; as his excellency is a foreigner, and a papist, he has no reason to rely on me for his justification; I shall only assure the world he is alive— but as he was bred to letters, and is master of a pen, let him use it in his own defence. In the mean time I shall present the publick with a faithful narrative of the ungenerous treatment and hard usage I have received from the virulent papers and malicious practices of this pretended astrologer.

A true and impartial account of the proceedings of Isaac Bickerstaff, Esq; against me—

The 28th of March, Anno Dom. 1708, being the night this sham-prophet had so impudently fix'd for my last, which made little impression on myself; but I cannot answer for my whole family; for my wife, with a concern more than usual, prevailed on me to take somewhat to sweat for a cold; and, between the hours of eight and nine, to go to bed: The maid, as she was warming my bed, with a curiosity natural to young wenches, runs to the window, and asks of one passing the street, who the bell toll'd for? Dr. Partridge, says he, that famous almanack-maker, who died suddenly this evening: The poor girl provoked, told him he ly'd like a rascal; the other very sedately reply'd, the sexton had so informed him, and if false, he was to blame for imposing upon a stranger. She asked a second, and a third, as they passed, and every one was in the same tone. Now I don't say these are accomplices to a certain astrological 'squire, and that one Bickerstaff might be sauntring thereabouts; because I will assert nothing here but what I dare attest, and plain matter of fact. My wife at this fell into a violent disorder; and I must own I was a little discomposed at the oddness of the accident. In the mean time one knocks at my door, Betty runs down, and opening, finds a sober grave person, who modestly enquires if this was Dr. Partridge's? She taking him for some cautious city-patient, that came at that time for privacy, shews him into the dining room. As soon as I could compose myself, I went to him, and was surprized to find my gentleman mounted on a table with a two-foot rule in his hand, measuring my walls, and taking the dimensions of the room. Pray sir, says I, not to interrupt you, have you any business with me? Only, sir, replies he, order the girl to bring me a better light, for this is but a very dim one. Sir, says I, my name is Partridge: Oh! the Doctor's brother, belike, cries he; the stair-case, I believe, and these two apartments hung in close mourning, will be sufficient, and only a strip of bays round the other rooms. The Doctor must needs die rich, he had great dealings in his way for many years; if he had no family coat, you had as good use the escutcheons of the company, they are as showish, and will look as magnificent as if he was descended from the blood royal. With that I assumed a great air of authority, and demanded who employ'd him, or how he came there? Why, I was sent, sir, by the Company of Undertakers, says he, and they were employed by the honest gentleman, who is executor to the good Doctor departed; and our rascally porter, I believe, is fallen fast asleep with the black cloth and sconces, or he had been here, and we might have been tacking up by this time. Sir, says I, pray be advis'd by a friend, and make the best of your speed out of my doors, for I hear my wife's voice, (which by the by, is pretty distinguishable) and in that corner of the room stands a good cudgel, which somebody has felt e're now; if that light in her hands, and she know the business you come about, without consulting the stars, I can assure you it will be employed very much to the detriment of your person. Sir, cries he, bowing with great civility, I perceive extreme grief for the loss of the Doctor disorders you a little at present, but early in the morning I'll wait on you with all necessary materials. Now I mention no Mr. Bickerstaff, nor do I say, that a certain star-gazing 'squire has been playing my executor before his time; but I leave the world to judge, and if he puts things and things fairly together, it won't be much wide of the mark.

Well, once more I got my doors clos'd, and prepar'd for bed, in hopes of a little repose after so many ruffling adventures; just as I was putting out my light in order to it, another bounces as hard as he can knock; I open the window, and ask who's there, and what he wants? I am Ned the sexton, replies he, and come to know whether the Doctor left any orders for a funeral sermon, and where he is to be laid, and whether his grave is to be plain or bricked? Why, sirrah, says I, you know me well enough; you know I am not dead, and how dare you affront me in this manner? Alack-a-day, replies the fellow, why 'tis in print, and the whole town knows you are dead; why, there's Mr. White the joiner is but fitting screws to your coffin, he'll be here with it in an instant: he was afraid you would have wanted it before this time. Sirrah, Sirrah, says I, you shall know tomorrow to your cost, that I am alive, and alive like to be. Why, 'tis strange, sir, says he, you should make such a secret of your death to us that are your neighbours; it looks as if you had a design to defraud the church of its dues; and let me tell you, for one that has lived so long by the heavens, that's unhandsomely done. Hist, Hist, says another rogue that stood by him, away Doctor, in your flannel gear as fast as you can, for here's a whole pack of dismals coming to you with their black equipage, and how indecent will it look for you to stand fright'ning folks at your window, when you should have been in your coffin this three hours? In short, what with undertakers, imbalmers, joiners, sextons, and your damn'd elegy hawkers, upon a late practitioner in physick and astrology, I got not one wink of sleep that night, nor scarce a moment's rest ever since. Now I doubt not but this villainous 'squire has the impudence to assert, that these are entirely strangers to him; he, good man, knows nothing of the matter, and honest Isaac Bickerstaff, I warrant you, is more a man of honour, than to be an accomplice with a pack of rascals, that walk the streets on nights, and disturb good people in their beds; but he is out, if he thinks the whole world is blind; for there is one John Partridge can smell a knave as far as Grubstreet,—tho' he lies in the most exalted garret, and writes himself 'Squire:—

But I'll keep my temper, and proceed in the narration.

I could not stir out of doors for the space of three months after this, but presently one comes up to me in the street; Mr. Partridge, that coffin you was last buried in I have not been yet paid for: Doctor, cries another dog, How d'ye think people can live by making of graves for nothing? Next time you die, you may e'en toll out the bell yourself for Ned. A third rogue tips me by the elbow, and wonders how I have the conscience to sneak abroad without paying my funeral expences. Lord, says one, I durst have swore that was honest Dr. Partridge, my old friend; but poor man, he is gone. I beg your pardon, says another, you look so like my old acquaintance that I used to consult on some private occasions; but, alack, he's gone the way of all flesh— Look, look, look, cries a third, after a competent space of staring at me, would not one think our neighbour the almanack-maker, was crept out of his grave to take t'other peep at the stars in this world, and shew how much he is improv'd in fortune-telling by having taken a journey to the other?

Nay, the very reader, of our parish, a good sober, discreet person, has sent two or three times for me to come and be buried decently, or send him sufficient reasons to the contrary, if I have been interr'd in any other parish, to produce my certificate, as the act requires. My poor wife is almost run distracted with being called Widow Partridge, when she knows its false; and once a term she is cited into the court, to take out letters of administration. But the greatest grievance is, a paultry quack, that takes up my calling just under my nose, and in his printed directions with N.B. says, He lives in the house of the late ingenious Mr. John Partridge, an eminent practitioner in leather, physick and astrology.

But to show how far the wicked spirit of envy, malice and resentment can hurry some men, my nameless old persecutor had provided me a monument at the stone-cutter's and would have erected it in the parish-church; and this piece of notorious and expensive villany had actually succeeded, had I not used my utmost interest with the vestry, where it was carried at last but by two voices, that I am still alive. That stratagem failing, out comes a long sable elegy, bedeck'd with hour-glasses, mattocks, sculls, spades, and skeletons, with an epitaph as confidently written to abuse me, and my profession, as if I had been under ground these twenty years.

And, after such barbarous treatment as this, can the world blame me, when I ask, What is become of the freedom of an Englishman? And where is the liberty and property that my old glorious friend came over to assert? We have drove popery out of the nation, and sent slavery to foreign climes. The arts only remain in bondage, when a man of science and character shall be openly insulted in the midst of the many useful services he is daily paying to the publick. Was it ever heard, even in Turkey or Algiers, that a state-astrologer was banter'd out of his life by an ignorant impostor, or bawl'd out of the world by a pack of villanous, deep-mouth'd hawkers? Though I print almanacks, and publish advertisements; though I produce certificates under the ministers and church-wardens hands I am alive, and attest the same on oath at quarter-sessions, out comes a full and true relation of the death and interment of John Partridge; Truth is bore down, attestations neglected, the testimony of sober persons despised, and a man is looked upon by his neighbours as if he had been seven years dead, and is buried alive in the midst of his friends and acquaintance.

Now can any man of common sense think it consistent with the honour of my profession, and not much beneath the dignity of a philosopher, to stand bawling before his own door?— Alive! Alive ho! The famous Dr. Partridge! No counterfeit, but all alive!— As if I had the twelve celestial monsters of the zodiac to shew within, or was forced for a livelihood to turn retailer to May and Bartholomew Fairs. Therefore, if Her Majesty would but graciously be pleased to think a hardship of this nature worthy her royal consideration, and the next parliament, in their great wisdom cast but an eye towards the deplorable case of their old philomath, that annually bestows his poetical good wishes on them, I am sure there is one Isaac Bickerstaff, Esq; would soon be truss'd up for his bloody predictions, and putting good subjects in terror of their lives: And that henceforward to murder a man by way of prophecy, and bury him in a printed letter, either to a lord or commoner, shall as legally entitle him to the present possession of Tyburn, as if he robb'd on the highway, or cut your throat in bed.

I shall demonstrate to the judicious, that France and Rome are at the bottom of this horrid conspiracy against me; and that culprit aforesaid is a popish emissary, has paid his visits to St. Germains, and is now in the measures of Lewis XIV. That in attempting my reputation, there is a general massacre of learning designed in these realms; and through my sides there is a wound given to all the Protestant almanack-makers in the universe.

Vivat Regina.

* * * * *

A vindication of Isaac Bickerstaff, Esq;

against what is objected to him by Mr. Partridge in his almanack for the present year 1709.

By the said Isaac Bickerstaff, Esq;

Written in the year 1709.

Mr. Partridge hath been lately pleased to treat me after a very rough manner, in that which is called, his almanack for the present year: Such usage is very undecent from one gentleman to another, and does not at all contribute to the discovery of truth, which ought to be the great end in all disputes of the learned. To call a man fool and villain, and impudent fellow, only for differing from him in a point meer speculative, is, in my humble opinion, a very improper style for a person of his education. I appeal to the learned world, whether in my last year's predictions I gave him the least provocation for such unworthy treatment. Philosophers have differed in all ages; but the discreetest among them have always differed as became philosophers. Scurrility and passion, in a controversy among scholars, is just so much of nothing to the purpose, and at best, a tacit confession of a weak cause: My concern is not so much for my own reputation, as that of the Republick of Letters, which Mr. Partridge hath endeavoured to wound through my sides. If men of publick spirit must be superciliously treated for their ingenious attempts, how will true useful knowledge be ever advanced? I wish Mr. Partridge knew the thoughts which foreign universities have conceived of his ungenerous proceedings with me; but I am too tender of his reputation to publish them to the world. That spirit of envy and pride, which blasts so many rising genius's in our nation, is yet unknown among professors abroad: The necessity of justifying myself will excuse my vanity, when I tell the reader that I have near a hundred honorary letters from several parts of Europe (some as far as Muscovy) in praise of my performance. Besides several others, which, as I have been credibly informed, were open'd in the post-office and never sent me. 'Tis true the Inquisition in Portugal was pleased to burn my predictions, and condem the author and readers of them; but I hope at the same time, it will be consider'd in how deplorable a state learning lies at present in that kingdom: And with the profoundest veneration for crown'd heads, I will presume to add, that it a little concerned His Majesty of Portugal, to interpose his authority in behalf of a scholar and a gentleman, the subject of a nation with which he is now in so strict an alliance. But the other kingdoms and states of Europe have treated me with more candor and generosity. If I had leave to print the Latin letters transmitted to me from foreign parts, they would fill a volume, and be a full defence against all that Mr. Partridge, or his accomplices of the Portugal Inquisition, will be able to object; who, by the way, are the only enemies my predictions have ever met with at home or abroad. But I hope I know better what is due to the honour of a learned correspondence in so tender a point. Yet some of those illustrious persons will perhaps excuse me from transcribing a passage or two in my own vindication. The most learned Monsieur Leibnits thus addresses to me his third letter: Illustrissimo Bickerstaffio Astrologiae instauratori, etc. Monsieur le Clerc, quoting my predictions in a treatise he published last year, is pleased to say, Ita nuperrime Bickerstaffius magnum illud Angliae fidus. Another great professor writing of me, has these words: Bickerstaffius, nobilis Anglus, Astrologorum hujusce Saeculi facile Princeps. Signior Magliabecchi, the Great Duke's famous library-keeper, spends almost his whole letter in compliments and praises. 'Tis true, the renowned Professor of Astronomy at Utrecht, seems to differ from me in one article; but it is in a modest manner, that becomes a philosopher; as, Pace tanti viri dixerim: And pag.55, he seems to lay the error upon the printer (as indeed it ought) and says, vel forsan error typographi, cum alioquin Bickerstaffius ver doctissimus, etc.

If Mr. Partridge had followed this example in the controversy between us, he might have spared me the trouble of justifying myself in so publick a manner. I believe few men are readier to own their errors than I, or more thankful to those who will please to inform me of them. But it seems this gentleman, instead of encouraging the progress of his own art, is pleased to look upon all attempts of that kind as an invasion of his province. He has been indeed so wise to make no objection against the truth of my predictions, except in one single point, relating to himself: And to demonstrate how much men are blinded by their own partiality, I do solemnly assure the reader, that he is the only person from whom I ever heard that objection offered; which consideration alone, I think, will take off all its weight.

With my utmost endeavours, I have not been able to trace above two objections ever made against the truth of my last year's prophecies: The first was of a French man, who was pleased to publish to the world, that the Cardinal de Noailles was still alive, notwithstanding the pretended prophecy of Monsieur Biquerstaffe: But how far a Frenchman, a papist, and an enemy is to be believed in his own case against an English Protestant, who is true to his government, I shall leave to the candid and impartial reader.

The other objection is the unhappy occasion of this discourse, and relates to an article in my predictions, which foretold the death of Mr. Partridge, to happen on March 29, 1708. This he is pleased to contradict absolutely in the almanack he has published for the present year, and in that ungentlemanly manner (pardon the expression) as I have above related. In that work he very roundly asserts, That he is not only now alive, but was likewise alive upon that very 29th of March, when I had foretold he should die. This is the subject of the present controversy between us; which I design to handle with all brevity, perspicuity, and calmness: In this dispute, I am sensible the eyes not only of England, but of all Europe, will be upon us; and the learned in every country will, I doubt not, take part on that side, where they find most appearance of reason and truth.

Without entering into criticisms of chronology about the hour of his death, I shall only prove that Mr. Partridge is not alive. And my first argument is thus: Above a thousand gentelmen having bought his almanacks for this year, merely to find what he said against me; at every line they read, they would lift up their eyes, and cry out, betwixt rage and laughter, "They were sure no man alive ever writ such damn'd stuff as this." Neither did I ever hear that opinion disputed: So that Mr. Partridge lies under a dilemma, either of disowning his almanack, or allowing himself to be "no man alive." But now if an uninformed carcase walks still about, and is pleased to call itself Partridge, Mr. Bickerstaff does not think himself any way answerable for that. Neither had the said carcase any right to beat the poor boy who happen'd to pass by it in the street, crying, "A full and true account of Dr. Partridge's death, etc."

Secondly, Mr. Partridge pretends to tell fortunes, and recover stolen goods; which all the parish says he must do by conversing with the devil and other evil spirits: And no wise man will ever allow he could converse personally with either, till after he was dead.

Thirdly, I will plainly prove him to be dead out of his own almanack for this year, and from the very passage which he produces to make us think him alive. He there says, "He is not only now alive, but was also alive on the very 29th of March, which I foretold he should die on": By this, he declares his opinion, that a man may be alive now, who was not alive a twelvemonth ago. And indeed, there lies the sophistry of this argument. He dares not assert, he was alive ever since that 29th of March, but that he is now alive, and was so on that day: I grant the latter; for he did not die till night, as appears by the printed account of his death, in a letter to a lord; and whether he is since revived I leave the world to judge. This indeed is perfect cavilling, and I am ashamed to dwell any longer upon it.

Fourthly, I will appeal to Mr. Partridge himself, whether it be probable I could have been so indiscreet, to begin my predictions with the only falsehood that ever was pretended to be in them; and this in an affair at home, where I had so many opportunities to be exact; and must have given such advantages against me to a person of Mr. Partridge's wit and learning, who, if he could possibly have raised one single objection more against the truth of my prophecies, would hardly have spared me.

And here I must take occasion to reprove the above mention'd writer of the relation of Mr. Partridge's death, in a letter to a lord; who was pleased to tax me with a mistake of four whole hours in my calculation of that event. I must confess, this censure pronounced with an air of certainty, in a matter that so nearly concerned me, and by a grave judicious author, moved me not a little. But tho' I was at that time out of town, yet several of my friends, whose curiosity had led them to be exactly informed (for as to my own part, having no doubt at all in the matter, I never once thought of it) assured me, I computed to something under half an hour: which (I speak my private opinion) is an error of no very great magnitude, that men should raise a clamour about it. I shall only say, it would not be amiss, if that author would henceforth be more tender of other men's reputations as well as his own. It is well there were no more mistakes of that kind; if there had, I presume he would have told me of them with as little ceremony.

There is one objection against Mr. Partridge's death, which I have sometimes met with, though indeed very slightly offered, That he still continues to write almanacks. But this is no more than what is common to all that profession; Gadbury, Poor Robin, Dove, Wing, and several others, do yearly publish their almanacks, though several of them have been dead since before the Revolution. Now the natural reason of this I take to be, that whereas it is the privilege of other authors to live after their deaths; almanack-makers are alone excluded, because their dissertations treating only upon the minutes as they pass, become useless as those go off. In consideration of which, Time, whose registers they are, gives them a lease in reversion, to continue their works after their death.

I should not have given the publick or myself the trouble of this vindication, if my name had not been made use of by several persons, to whom I never lent it; one of which, a few days ago, was pleased to father on me a new sett of predictions. But I think those are things too serious to be trifled with. It grieved me to the heart, when I saw my labours, which had cost me so much thought and watching, bawl'd about by common hawkers, which I only intended for the weighty consideration of the gravest persons. This prejudiced the world so much at first, that several of my friends had the assurance to ask me whether I were in jest? To which I only answered coldly, that the event would shew. But it is the talent of our age and nation, to turn things of the greatest importance into ridicule. When the end of the year had verified all my predictions, out comes Mr. Partridge's almanack, disputing the point of his death; so that I am employed, like the general who was forced to kill his enemies twice over, whom a necromancer had raised to life. If Mr. Partridge has practised the same experiment upon himself, and be again alive, long may he continue so; that does not in the least contradict my veracity: But I think I have clearly proved, by invincible demonstration, that he died at farthest within half an hour of the time I foretold, and not four hours sooner, as the above-mentioned author, in his letter to a lord, hath maliciously suggested, with design to blast my credit, by charging me with so gross a mistake.

* * * * *

A famous prediction of Merlin, the British wizard.

Written above a thousand years ago, and relating to the year 1709, with explanatory notes.

Last year was publish'd a paper of predictions, pretended to be written by one Isaac Bickerstaff, Esq; but the true design of it was to ridicule the art of astrology, and expose its professors as ignorant or impostors. Against this imputation, Dr. Partridge hath vindicated himself in his almanack for that year.

For a farther vindication of this famous art, I have thought fit to present the world with the following prophecy. The original is said to be of the famous Merlin, who lived about a thousand years ago; and the following translation is two hundred years old, for it seems to be written near the end of Henry the Seventh's reign. I found it in an old edition of Merlin's Prophecies, imprinted at London by John Hawkins in the year 1530, page 39. I set it down word for word in the old orthography, and shall take leave to subjoin a few explanatory notes.

Seven and Ten addyd to Nyne,
Of Fraunce her Woe this is the Sygne,
Tamys Rivere twys y-frozen,
Walke sans wetyng Shoes ne Hozen.
Then comyth foorthe, ich understonde,
From Town of Stoffe to farryn Londe,
An herdye Chyftan, woe the Morne
To Fraunce, that evere he was born.
Than shall the fyshe beweyle his Bosse;
Nor shall grin Berrys make up the Losse.
Yonge Symnele shall again miscarrye:
And Norways Pryd again shall marrye.
And from the tree where Blosums feele,
Ripe Fruit shall come, and all is wele,
Reaums shall daunce Honde in Honde,
And it shall be merrye in old Inglonde,
Then old Inglonde shall be no more,
And no man shall be sorre therefore.
Geryon shall have three Hedes agayne,
Till Hapsburge makyth them but twayne.

Explanatory notes.

Seven and Ten. This line describes the year when these events shall happen. Seven and ten makes seventeen, which I explain seventeen hundred, and this number added to nine, makes the year we are now in; for it must be understood of the natural year, which begins the first of January.

Tamys Rivere twys, etc. The River Thames, frozen twice in one year, so as men to walk on it, is a very signal accident, which perhaps hath not fallen out for several hundred years before, and is the reason why some astrologers have thought that this prophecy could never be fulfilled, because they imagine such a thing would never happen in our climate.

From Town of Stoffe, etc. This is a plain designation of the Duke of Marlborough: One kind of stuff used to fatten land is called marle, and every body knows that borough is a name for a town; and this way of expression is after the usual dark manner of old astrological predictions.

Then shall the Fyshe, etc. By the fish, is understood the Dauphin of France, as their kings eldest sons are called: 'Tis here said, he shall lament the loss of the Duke of Burgundy, called the Bosse, which is an old English word for hump-shoulder, or crook-back, as that Duke is known to be; and the prophecy seems to mean, that he should be overcome or slain. By the green berrys, in the next line, is meant the young Duke of Berry, the Dauphin's third son, who shall not have valour or fortune enough to supply the loss of his eldest brother.

Yonge Symnele, etc. By Symnele is meant the pretended Prince of Wales, who, if he offers to attempt anything against England, shall miscarry as he did before. Lambert Symnele is the name of a young man, noted in our histories for personating the son (as I remember) of Edward the fourth.

And Norway's Pryd, etc. I cannot guess who is meant by Norway's Pride, perhaps the reader may, as well as the sense of the two following lines.

Reaums shall, etc. Reums, or, as the word is now, realms, is the old name for kingdoms: And this is a very plain prediction of our happy Union, with the felicities that shall attend it. It is added that Old England shall be no more, and yet no man shall be sorry for it. And indeed, properly speaking, England is now no more, for the whole island is one Kingdom, under the name of Britain.

Geryon shall, etc. This prediction, tho' somewhat obscure, is wonderfully adapt. Geryon is said to have been a king of Spain, whom Hercules slew. It was a fiction of the poets, that he had three heads, which the author says he shall have again: That is, Spain shall have three kings; which is now wonderfully verified; for besides the King of Portugal, which properly is part of Spain, there are now two rivals for Spain, Charles and Philip: But Charles being descended fro the Count of Hapsburgh, founder of the Austrian family, shall soon make those heads but two; by overturning Philip, and driving him out of Spain.

Some of these predictions are already fulfilled; and it is highly probable the rest may be in due time; and, I think, I have not forced the words, by my explication, into any other sense than what they will naturally bear. If this be granted, I am sure it must be also allow'd, that the author (whoever he were) was a person of extraordinary sagacity; and that astrology brought to such perfection as this, is by no means an art to be despised, whatever Mr. Bickerstaff, or other merry gentlemen are pleased to think. As to the tradition of these lines having been writ in the original by Merlin, I confess I lay not much weight upon it: But it is enough to justify their authority, that the book from whence I have transcrib'd them, was printed 170 years ago, as appears by the title-page. For the satisfaction of any gentleman, who may be either doubtful of the truth, or curious to be inform'd; I shall give order to have the very book sent to the printer of this paper, with directions to let anybody see it that pleases, because I believe it is pretty scarce.

*   *   *   *   *

Dr. John Arbuthnot and Alexander Pope

Annus Mirabilis: or, The wonderful effects of the approaching conjunction of the planets Jupiter, Mars, and Saturn.

By Mart. Scriblerus, Philomath.

In nova fert animus mutatas dicere formas corpora. . . .

I suppose every body is sufficiently appriz'd of, and duly prepar'd for, the famous conjunction to be celebrated the 29th of this instant December, 1722, foretold by all the sages of antiquity, under the name of the Annus Mirabilis, or the metamorphostical conjunction: a word which denotes the mutual transformation of sexes, (the effect of that configuration of the celestial bodies) the human males being turn'd into females, and the human females into males.

The Egyptians have represented this great transformation by several significant hieroglyphicks, particularly one very remarkable. There are carv'd upon an obelisk, a barber and a midwife; the barber delivers his razor to the midwife, and she her swadling-cloaths to the barber. Accordingly Thales Milesius (who like the rest of his countrymen, borrow'd his learning from the Egyptians) after having computed the time of this famous conjunction, "Then," says he, "shall men and women mutually exchange the pangs of shaving and child-bearing."

Anaximander modestly describes this metamorphosis in mathematical terms: "Then," says he, "shall the negative quantity of the women be turn'd into positive, their − into +;" (i.e.) their minus into plus.

Plato not only speaks of this great change, but describes all the preparations towards it. "Long before the bodily transformation, (says he) nature shall begin the most difficult part of her work, by changing the ideas and inclinations of the two sexes: Men shall turn effeminate, and women manly; wives shall domineer, and husbands obey; ladies shall ride a horseback, dress'd like cavaliers; princes and nobles appear in night-rails and petticoats; men shall squeak upon theatres with female voices, and women corrupt virgins; lords shall knot and cut paper; and even the northern people. . . :" A Greek phrase (which for modesty's sake I forbear to translate) which denotes a vice too frequent amongst us.

That the Ministry foresaw this great change, is plain from the Callico-Act; whereby it is now become the occupation of women all over England, to convert their useless female habits into beds, window-curtains, chairs, and joint-stools; undressing themselves (as it were) before their transformation.

The philosophy of this transformation will not seem surprizing to people who search into the bottom of things. Madam Bourignon, a devout French lady, has shewn us, how man was at first created male and female in one individual, having the faculty of propagation within himself: A circumstance necessary to the state of innocence, wherein a man's happiness was not to depend upon the caprice of another. It was not till after he had made a faux pas, that he had his female mate. Many such transformations of individuals have been well attested; particularly one by Montaigne, and another by the late Bishop of Salisbury. From all which it appears, that this system of male and female has already undergone and may hereafter suffer, several alterations. Every smatterer in anatomy knows, that a woman is but an introverted man; a new fusion and flatus will turn the hollow bottom of a bottle into a convexity; but I forbear, (for the sake of my modest men-readers, who are in a few days to be virgins.)

In some subjects, the smallest alterations will do: some men are sufficiently spread about the hips, and contriv'd with female softness, that they want only the negative quantity to make them buxom wenches; and there are women who are, as it were, already the ebauche of a good sturdy man. If nature cou'd be puzzl'd, it will be how to bestow the redundant matter of the exuberant bubbies that now appear about town, or how to roll out the short dapper fellows into well-siz'd women.

This great conjunction will begin to operate on Saturday the 29th instant. Accordingly, about eight at night, as Senezino shall begin at the Opera, si videte, he shall be observ'd to make an unusual motion; upon which the audience will be affected with a red suffusion over their countenance: And because a strong succession of the muscles of the belly is necessary towards performing this great operation, both sexes will

JONATHAN SWIFT

be thrown into a profuse involuntary laughter. Then (to use the modest terms of Anaximander) shall negative quantity be turn'd into positive, etc. Time never beheld, nor will it ever assemble, such a number of untouch'd virgins within those walls! but alas! such will be the impatience and curiosity of people to act in their new capacity, that many of them will be compleated men and women that very night. To prevent the disorders that may happen upon this occasion, is the chief design of this paper.

Gentlemen have begun already to make use of this conjunction to compass their filthy purposes. They tell the ladies forsooth, that it is only parting with a perishable commodity, hardly of so much value as a callico under-petticoat; since, like its mistress, it will be useless in the form it is now in. If the ladies have no regard to the dishonour and immorality of the action, I desire they will consider, that nature who never destroys her own productions, will exempt big-belly'd women till the time of their lying-in; so that not to be transformed, will be the same as to be pregnant. If they don't think it worth while to defend a fortress that is to be demolish'd in a few days, let them reflect that it will be a melancholy thing nine months hence, to be brought to bed of a bastard; a posthumous bastard as it were, to which the quondam father can be no more than a dry nurse.

This wonderful transformation is the instrument of nature, to balance matters between the sexes. The cruelty of scornful mistresses shall be return'd; the slighted maid shall grow into an imperious gallant, and reward her undoer with a big belly, and a bastard.

It is hardly possible to imagine the revolutions that this wonderful phaenomenon will occasion over the face of the earth. I long impatiently to see the proceedings of the Parliament of Paris, as to the title of succession to the crown, this being a case not provided for by the salique law. There will be no preventing disorders amongst friars and monks; for certainly vows of chastity do not bind but under the sex in which they were made. The same will hold good with marriages, tho' I think it will be a scandal amongst Protestants for husbands and wives to part, since there remains still a possibility to perform the debitus conjugale, by the husband being femme couverte. I submit it to the judgment of the gentlemen of the long robe, whether this transformation does not discharge all suits of rapes?

The Pope must undergo a new groping; but the false prophet Mahomet has contriv'd matters well for his successors; for as the Grand Signior has now a great many fine women, he will then have as many fine young gentelmen, at his devotion.

These are surprizing scenes; but I beg leave to affirm, that the solemn operations of nature are subjects of contemplation, not of ridicule. Therefore I make it my earnest request to the merry fellows, and giggling girls about town, that they would not put themselves in a high twitter, when they go to visit a general lying-in of his first child; his officers serving as midwives, nurses and rockers dispensing caudle; or if they behold the reverend prelates dressing the heads and airing the linnen at court, I beg they will remember that these offices must be fill'd with people of the greatest regularity, and best characters. For the same reason, I am sorry that a certain prelate, who notwithstanding his confinement (in December 1723), still preserves his healthy, chearful countenance, cannot come in time to be a nurse at court.

I likewise earnestly intreat the maids of honour, (then ensigns and captains of the guard) that, at their first setting out, they have some regard to their former station, and do not run wild through all the infamous houses about town: That the present grooms of the bed-chamber (then maids of honour) would not eat chalk and lime in their green-sickness: And in general, that the men would remember they are become retromingent, and not by inadvertency lift up against walls and posts.

Petticoats will not be burdensome to the clergy; but balls and assemblies will be indecent for some time.

As for you, coquettes, bawds, and chamber-maids, (the future ministers, plenipotentiaries, and cabinet-counsellors to the princes of the earth,) manage the great intrigues that will be committed to your charge, with your usual secrecy and conduct; and the affairs of your masters will go better than ever.

O ye exchange women! (our right worshipful representatives that are to be) be not so griping in the sale of your ware as your predecessors, but consider that the nation, like a spend-thrift heir, has run out: Be likewise a little more continent in your tongues than you are at present, else the length of debates will spoil your dinners.

You housewifely good women, who now preside over the confectionary, (henceforth commissioners of the Treasury) be so good as to dispense the sugar-plumbs of the Government with a more impartial and frugal hand.

Ye prudes and censorious old maids, (the hopes of the Bench) exert but your usual talent of finding faults, and the laws will be strictly executed; only I would not have you proceed upon such slender evidences as you have done hitherto.

It is from you, eloquent oyster-merchants of Billingsgate, (just ready to be called to the Bar, and quoif'd like your sister-serjants,) that we expect the shortening the time, and lessening the expences of law-suits: For I think you are observ'd to bring your debates to a short issue; and even custom will restrain you from taking the oyster, and leaving only the shell to your client.

O ye physicians, (who in the figure of old women are to clean the tripe in the markets) scour it as effectually as you have done that of your patients, and the town will fare most deliciously on Saturdays.

I cannot but congratulate human nature, upon this happy transformation; the only expedient left to restore the liberties and tranquillity of mankind. This is so evident, that it is almost an affront to common sense to insist upon the proof: If there can be any such stupid creature as to doubt it, I desire he will make but the following obvious reflection. There are in Europe alone, at present, about a million of sturdy fellows, under the denomination of standing forces, with arms in their hands: That those are masters of the lives, liberties and fortunes of all the rest, I believe no body will deny. It is no less true in fact, that reams of paper, and above a square mile of skins of vellum have been employ'd to no purpose, to settle peace among those sons of violence. Pray, who is he that will say unto them, Go and disband yourselves? But lo! by this transformation it is done at once, and the halcyon days of publick tranquillity return: For neither the military temper nor discipline can taint the soft sex for a whole age to come: Bellaque matribus invisa, War odious to mothers, will not grow immediately palatable in their paternal state.

Nor will the influence of this transformation be less in family tranquillity, than it is in national. Great faults will be amended, and frailties forgiven, on both sides. A wife who has been disturb'd with late hours, and choak'd with the hautgout of a sot, will remember her sufferings, and avoid the temptations; and will, for the same reason, indulge her mate in his female capacity in some passions, which she is sensible from experience are natural to the sex. Such as vanity of fine cloaths, being admir'd, etc. And how tenderly must she use her mate under the breeding qualms and labour-pains which she hath felt her self? In short, all unreasonable demands upon husbands must cease, because they are already satisfy'd from natural experience that they are impossible.

That the ladies may govern the affairs of the world, and the gentlemen those of their household, better than either of them have hitherto done, is the hearty desire of, Their most sincere well-wisher, M.S.

A Note About the Author

Jonathan Swift (1667–1745) was an Irish poet and satirical writer. When the spread of Catholicism in Ireland became prevalent, Swift moved to England, where he lived and worked as a writer. Due to the controversial nature of his work, Swift often wrote under pseudonyms. In addition to his poetry and satirical prose, Swift also wrote for political pamphlets and since many of his works provided political commentary this was a fitting career stop for Swift. When he returned to Ireland, he was ordained as a priest in the Anglican church. Despite this, his writings stirred controversy about religion and prevented him from advancing in the clergy.

A Note from the Publisher

Spanning many genres, from non-fiction essays to literature classics to children's books and lyric poetry, Mint Edition books showcase the master works of our time in a modern new package. The text is freshly typeset, is clean and easy to read, and features a new note about the author in each volume. Many books also include exclusive new introductory material. Every book boasts a striking new cover, which makes it as appropriate for collecting as it is for gift giving. Mint Edition books are only printed when a reader orders them, so natural resources are not wasted. We're proud that our books are never manufactured in excess and exist only in the exact quantity they need to be read and enjoyed.

Discover more of your favorite classics with Bookfinity™.

- Track your reading with custom book lists.
- Get great book recommendations for your personalized Reader Type.
- Add reviews for your favorite books.
- AND MUCH MORE!

Visit **bookfinity.com** and take the fun Reader Type quiz to get started.

Enjoy our classic and modern companion pairings!

www.ingramcontent.com/pod-product-compliance
Lightning Source LLC
Chambersburg PA
CBHW020610130626
46552CB00007B/3128